D1541752

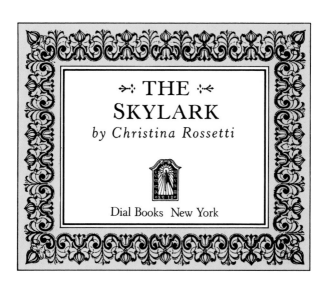

❧ THE ❧
SKYLARK
by *Christina Rossetti*

Dial Books New York

Published by Dial Books 1992
A Division of Penguin Books USA Inc.
375 Hudson Street
New York, New York 10014

Conceived and produced by Breslich & Foss, London
Copyright © 1991 by Breslich & Foss
All rights reserved
Printed in Singapore

Designed by Nigel Partridge

1 3 5 7 9 10 8 6 4 2

ISBN 0-8037-1143-3
Library of Congress Catalog Card Number: 91-13112

CHRISTINA ROSSETTI
1830–1894

Christina Georgina Rossetti was born in London, where she lived with her Italian father, her mother, and two brothers, one of whom was the famous painter Dante Gabriel Rossetti. She was extremely beautiful, but very shy, and never married although she was asked several times. She wrote many stories, hymns, and poems including a collection for children entitled *Sing-Song*. She died at the age of sixty-four.

⤞ THE ⤝
SKYLARK
by
Christina
Rossetti

THE earth was green, the sky was blue:
I saw and heard one sunny morn

A skylark hang between the two,

A singing speck above the corn;

A stage below, in gay accord,

White butterflies danced on the wing,

AND still the singing skylark soared,

And silent sank, and soared to sing.

THE cornfield stretched a tender green

To right and left beside my walks;

I knew he had a nest unseen

Somewhere among the million stalks.

ᴀɴᴅ as I paused to hear his song,

While swift the sunny moments slid,

PERHAPS his mate sat listening long,
And listened longer than I did.

ACKNOWLEDGMENTS

All pictures are courtesy of Fine Art Photographic
Library, London.

THE PAINTERS
Oliver Clare (nineteenth/twentieth century)
Emile Czech (nineteenth century)
Arthur Foster (fl. 1880–1905)
Frank Topham (1838–1924)
W. Scott Myles (nineteenth/twentieth century)
F. Blacklock (1872–1924)
Endpapers: John White (1851–1933)
Front Cover: John Clayton Adams (1840–1906)